I WANNA BE A

Cowgirl

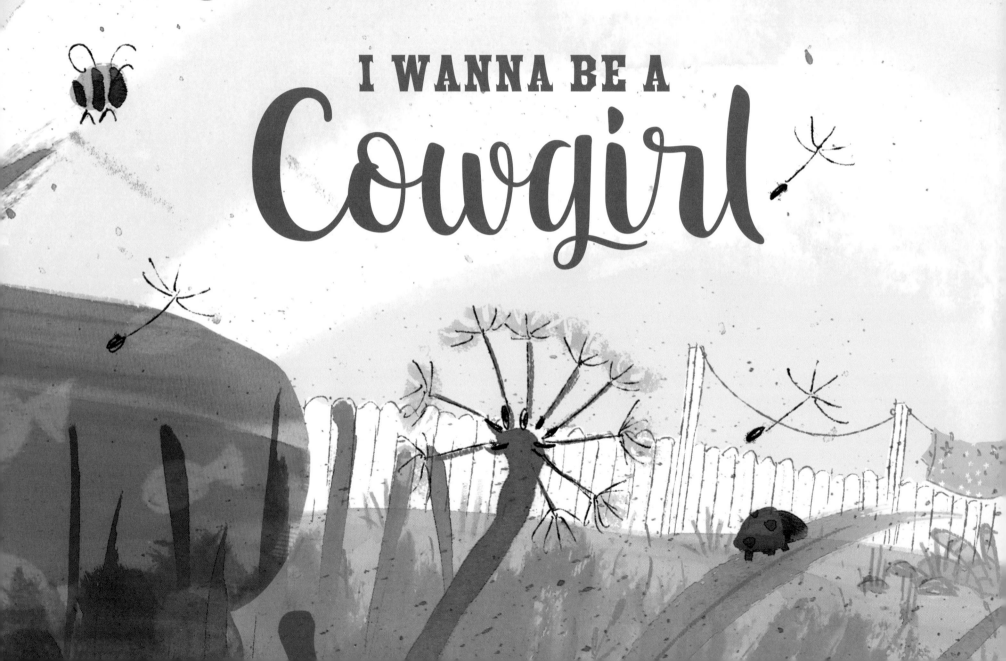

written by
Angela DiTerlizzi

illustrated by
Elizabet Vukovic

I WANNA BE A
Cowgirl

Beach Lane Books

New York   London   Toronto   Sydney   New Delhi

Way out west, the warm winds blow.

The grass grows high, the sun hangs low.

I'll find a ranch, there I'll go . . .

and I'll become a cowgirl.

I'll wear my boots and spurs and hat.

I'll say so long to my barn cat.

A cowgirl's life is where it's at.

I'm gonna be a cowgirl.

I'll hop atop my horse and ride,
my trusty pup right by my side.

I'll gallop fast, and with each stride . . .

I'll know that I'm a cowgirl.

I'll check in on my chicken coops.

I'll make my rope do loop-de-loops—

a lasso spinnin', makin' hoops.

It's tough to be a cowgirl!

I'll milk the cows.

I'll shear the sheep.

I'll take a bath
right in the creek!

It's fun to be a cowgirl.

I'll mosey in to rest my head.

I'll get some grub, unroll my bed.

I'll be tired, but warm and fed.

I love to be a cowgirl.

Home on the range, I'll close my eyes.

I'll snuggle up until sunrise.

I'll sleep beneath the starry skies.

And dream . . .

that I'm a cowgirl!

For Dolly Parton—
the first cowgirl I ever wanted to be
—A. D.

For Jackie and Max
—E. V.

BEACH LANE BOOKS • An imprint of Simon & Schuster Children's Publishing Division
• 1230 Avenue of the Americas, New York, New York 10020 • Text copyright © 2017 by Angela
DiTerlizzi • Illustrations copyright © 2017 by Elizabet Vukovic • All rights reserved, including
the right of reproduction in whole or in part in any form. • BEACH LANE BOOKS is a trademark
of Simon & Schuster, Inc. • For information about special discounts for bulk purchases, please
contact Simon & Schuster Special Sales at 1-866-506-1949 or business@simonandschuster.com.
• The Simon & Schuster Speakers Bureau can bring authors to your live event. For more
information or to book an event, contact the Simon & Schuster Speakers Bureau at 1-866-248-3049
or visit our website at www.simonspeakers.com.
Book design by Lauren Rille
The text for this book was set in Clarendon.
The illustrations for this book were rendered in watercolor, gouache,
colored pencil, and Photoshop.
Manufactured in China
0817 SCP
First Edition
10 9 8 7 6 5 4 3 2 1
CIP data for this book is available from the Library of Congress.
ISBN 978-1-4814-5299-1
ISBN 978-1-4814-5300-4 (eBook)